P9-CRD-863

Welcome to ALADDIN QUIX!

If you are looking for fast, fun-to-read stories with colorful characters, lots of kid-friendly humor, easy-to-follow action, entertaining story lines, and lively illustrations, then **ALADDIN QUIX** is for you!

But wait, there's more!

If you're also looking for stories with tables of contents; word lists; about-the-book questions; 64, 80, or 96 pages; short chapters; short paragraphs; and large fonts, then **ALADDIN QUIX** is *definitely* for you!

ALADDIN QUIX: The next step between ready to reads and longer, more challenging chapter books, for readers five to eight years old.

Read more ALADDIN QUIX books!

Our Principal Is a Frog!
by Stephanie Calmenson

Royal Sweets: A Royal Rescue
by Helen Perelman

A Miss Mallard Mystery: Texas Trail to Calamity
by Robert Quackenbush

A Miss Mallard Mystery

DIG TO DISASTER

ROBERT QUACKENBUSH

ALADDIN QUIX

New York London Toronto Sydney New Delhi

This book is a work of fiction. Any references to historical events, real people, or real places are used fictitiously. Other names, characters, places, and events are products of the author's imagination, and any resemblance to actual events or places or persons, living or dead, is entirely coincidental.

ALADDIN QUIX
Simon & Schuster Children's Publishing Division
1230 Avenue of the Americas, New York, New York 10020
This Aladdin QUIX hardcover edition May 2018

Also available in an Aladdin QUIX paperback edition.

Designed by Nina Simoneaux
The illustrations for this book were rendered in pen and ink and wash.
The text of this book was set in Archer Medium.
Manufactured in the United States of America 0418 FFG
2 4 6 8 10 9 7 5 3 1
The Library of Congress has cataloged a previous edition as follows:
Quackenbush, Robert M.
Dig to disaster.
"A Miss Mallard Mystery."
Summary: When the terrifying headless demon of Kimbu Tacka threatens an archaeological expedition in the South American jungle, Miss Mallard uses her detective skills to unravel the clues and uncover the true villain.
[1. Ducks—Fiction. 2. Mystery and detective stories.] I. Title.
PZ7.Q16Dj [Fic.] 82-7531 AACR2
ISBN 978-1-5344-1313-9 (hc)
ISBN 978-1-5344-1312-2 (pbk)
ISBN 978-1-5344-1314-6 (eBook)

First for Piet and Margie and J.R. Bray,

and now for Emma and Aidan

Cast of Characters

Miss Mallard: World-famous ducktective

Harold Scoter: A tourist, the same as Miss Mallard, on the trip to Kimbu Tacka

Dr. Peter Dusty Duck: Well-known archaeologist and explorer

Victor Shoveller: Assistant to Dr. Duck

Morris Goosander: An artist

Max Butterball: Photographer

Hester Spoonbill: Journalist

What's in Miss Mallard's Bag?

Miss Mallard has many detective tools she brings with her on her adventures around the world.

In her knitting bag she usually has:

- Newspaper clippings
- Knitting needles and yarn
- A magnifying glass
- A flashlight
- A mirror
- A travel guide
- Chocolates for her nephew

Contents

1

A Narrow Escape

Miss Mallard, the world-famous ducktective, ran through the rain across the narrow rope bridge.

The bridge swayed wildly in the wind. She was sure it would **collapse** any minute.

Just as she made it to the other side of the gorge, a cable broke! The bridge fell in a tangled heap one hundred feet below.

"That was close," said Miss Mallard. She dived under a fern for shelter and crashed into Harold Scoter.

"Watch it!" cried Scoter. "Haven't I endured enough on this miserable trek without being knocked about, too?"

"I'm sorry," said Miss Mallard, "but I didn't see you. I had a

narrow escape. Just as I got across the bridge, the whole thing collapsed from under me. I can't imagine what happened."

"Well, I can," said Scoter. "I've been saying it all along. This **expedition** is haunted! No one is safe!"

"How can you say that, Harold?" asked Miss Mallard in surprise. "We are with such a fine and experienced group. You and I are the only tourists. There's . . .

Dr. Peter Dusty Duck, the well-known archaeologist and explorer, **Victor Shoveller**, his assistant, **Morris Goosander**, an artist, **Max Butterball**, a photographer, and **Hester Spoonbill**, a journalist."

Miss Mallard continued, "They are all perfectly suited to go digging for the lost city of Kimbu Tacka. They know all the rules for safety.

"Certainly not one of them

believes a headless demon is after us."

Miss Mallard looked Scoter straight in the eye. "And neither should you!" she proclaimed.

"They'll change their minds soon enough. You'll see," said Scoter. "Just as I have. **Mark my words!**"

Suddenly the rain stopped.

"Listen up, everyone, let's move on," called Dr. Dusty Duck to the group.

Harold Scoter ran out from under the fern to tell Dr. Dusty Duck all about the collapsed bridge.

"You see!" he cried. "Another disaster! Just like yesterday when the boulder rolled down the hill and nearly crushed poor Hester Spoonbill. We *must* turn back!"

"These things happen," said Dr. Dusty Duck.

"You said that yesterday!" said Scoter.

"I know," answered Dr. Dusty Duck.

Dr. Dusty Duck went over to Miss Mallard. "What's this I hear?" he asked. "Are you all right?"

"I'm fine," answered Miss Mallard. "But I'm afraid the bridge is gone."

"Don't worry about it," said Dr. Dusty Duck. "Victor will make us a new one when we return from Kimbu Tacka."

Miss Mallard asked, "Do you

suppose all these accidents have anything to do with the **threatening** messages? The ones that made you ask me to come on this dig?"

"You mean those letters signed 'The Headless Demon'?" asked Dr. Dusty Duck. "I don't think there is any connection. These things happen."

2

Adrift on the River

Dr. Dusty Duck told everyone to form a line, and the expedition continued on toward the lost city of Kimbu Tacka.

All morning the party waddled along a narrow path through the

dark jungle. At last they came to a small clearing of bamboo huts by a river. Friendly ducks came out to greet them.

Dr. Dusty Duck looked at his maps and said, "This is as far as we can go on foot. The river is dangerous, with rapids and whirl-pools and waterfalls. We must travel the rest of the way by dug-out canoe."

They all squeezed into a dug-out and cast themselves adrift on the river.

The dugout tore downstream, bouncing along over rapids and swift **undercurrents**. The oars were useless except to keep it from crashing into the cliffs on each bank.

Suddenly the dugout sprang a leak. Everyone began furiously bailing water with hats, shovels, and canteen cups. Just as the dugout was about to sink, Dr. Dusty Duck yelled at Victor to guide it to shore.

"We're safe!" he shouted.

"Not much farther now!"

"Whew!" said Miss Mallard as they all climbed out of the dugout. "That was quite an experience."

"Experience!" cried Harold Scoter. "Experience! That is the **understatement** of the year. We nearly drowned!"

"**Nonsense!** We're ducks," said Miss Mallard briskly.

"Well, I'm convinced that this expedition is spooked," Harold Scoter **retorted**. "I plan to sue as

soon as we return to civilization—if we ever do."

"These things happen," said Dr. Dusty Duck. "Come this way."

They all adjusted their knap-sacks. Then they followed Dr. Dusty Duck and Victor, who were cutting a path through the dense forest up a hill.

Dr. Dusty Duck kept looking at his map and **muttering** to himself.

At last the expedition reached

the top of the hill. All eyes widened with surprise and wonder at what they saw.

Before them was the lost city of Kimbu Tacka.

3

A Headless Demon

"We found it!" cried Dr. Dusty Duck. "And look! This stone tells the date Kimbu Tacka was built. In the Mayan calendar it is nine, eleven, zero, zero, zero."

"Phooey!" said Scoter.

"It actually says nine, thirteen, zero, zero, zero. Don't you know anything?"

"So it does," said Dr. Dusty Duck. "Well, let's set up camp at the base of that temple and have supper. We'll start digging and exploring in the morning."

Underneath the full moon, the camp was set up in a circle. After supper everyone gathered around the fire to hear Dr. Dusty Duck's stories. He told about the history of the country.

"Spanish conquerors came to the land," he said, "and **plundered** and **destroyed** the ancient cities. That was over four hundred years ago. Only Kimbu Tacka survived."

Dr. Dusty Duck continued. "Legend tells us that when the Spaniards came here, they were frightened away by a headless demon riding on a giant armadillo."

"It's not legend—it's fact!" cried Scoter. "This expedition proved that. It's spooked by the demon, I tell you. Enough of this. I'm going to bed."

"You do that," said Max Butterball. "You're a pain in the tail feathers."

"Yeah!" snorted Morris Goosander.

"Gentlemen!" cried Dr. Dusty Duck. "Gentlemen! Need I warn you that differences can ruin an expedition?"

Scoter snorted and stomped off. But no sooner had he left than he was heard quacking loudly.

Everyone ran to see what was the matter.

"Something touched me!" cried Scoter. "I felt a cold, **clammy** wing brush against my face just as I lay down! It was the demon, I'm sure of it!"

"These things happen," said Dr. Dusty Duck. "Perhaps it was the night wind that brushed your cheek. Let's all go to bed before we begin imagining things."

Everyone was a bit nervous after that.

They all climbed into their hammocks and were soon fast asleep.

But not for long.

4

Midnight Horror

At midnight there came the loud blare of a jungle horn from somewhere out in the forest.

Miss Mallard awoke with a start. She sat bolt upright in her hammock and looked around. She

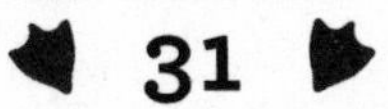

could see clearly in the moonlight that the others had also heard the frightening sound.

She saw that they were all sitting up in their hammocks looking scared, except for Scoter. He was hiding under his blanket.

"What *was* that?" asked Miss Mallard.

"The demon! It was the demon!" cried Victor.

Just then they heard movement in the brush. Out crashed a huge armadillo. Something

was riding on its back. It was the headless demon!

Everyone watched in horror as the armadillo raced twice around the campfire and then vanished into the forest.

"The demon! It was the demon!" Victor repeated.

"Get a hold of yourself!" cried Dr. Dusty Duck, shaking his assistant by the shoulders. "Don't you see that none of this is possible? How could a duck live—much less ride around on an armadillo—without a head?"

The shaking quieted Victor down. "Thanks," he said.

Dr. Dusty Duck turned to the others, who were still in a state of shock.

"Is everyone okay?" he asked.

"We should see about Harold Scoter," said Miss Mallard. "He was buried under his blanket. I hope he hasn't **smothered**."

They ran to Scoter's hammock and tore off the blanket. They found Scoter gasping for breath.

"It looks like we got here just in time," said Dr. Dusty Duck. "Thanks to you, Miss Mallard."

"Yeah, thanks, Miss Mallard," said Butterball and Goosander **sarcastically**.

No one slept the rest of the night.

The Investigation

At dawn there was talk of returning to civilization.

“But these things happen,” said Dr. Dusty Duck. “I am sure there is a reasonable explanation for what happened last night.”

Dr. Dusty Duck pleaded with the group. "We can't turn back now. There are pictures to be taken, drawings to be made, and ancient pottery to be unearthed. Just one more day, then I promise we will head back."

"Stop!" said Scoter. "I say we go back now. This Kimbu Tacka expedition is cursed."

Then Hester Spoonbill quacked, "This is the find of the century! We can't leave now without some proof we were really here!"

It was finally agreed that everyone would stay for one more day. They all split up to explore the ruins. Harold Scoter stayed behind to catch up on his sleep.

Miss Mallard went off to do another kind of exploring. She wanted to check into the raid by the headless demon and to look for clues.

She went to the spot where the demon had disappeared the night before. She saw some tire tracks on the ground.

"**Ooooh!** What's this?" she thought. "No one has a bicycle on our expedition."

She followed the tire tracks. They ended at the foot of a mountain.

Miss Mallard was puzzled. She sat down on a rock to study the situation. As soon as she did, the side of the mountain opened up!

Inside the mountain Miss Mallard saw digging tools, piles of treasure, and a painted cloth armadillo covering a bicycle!

"Well, I'll be!" said Miss Mallard. "A secret treasure dig!"

She jumped up from the rock, and the mountain slid shut again.

"Hmmm!" said Miss Mallard. "Now I understand what's been going on. But who is behind this?"

Suddenly she remembered something!

She went back to camp to wait for the others to return. While she was waiting, she dug through the knitting bag in her knapsack and found her clipping file.

Z Z Z

In the file she located a list of archaeologists who were digging in Central America. She came to a name on the list she recognized.

"Hmmm," she said to herself. "I am about to snare a demon."

6

The Capture

When the others came back to camp, Miss Mallard said nothing about what she had discovered.

At nightfall everyone packed for their early morning **departure** and climbed into their hammocks.

Miss Mallard waited until she was sure all was quiet. Then she went into action.

She quietly crept from her hammock, taking a ball of her yarn with her. She looked around to make sure no one had seen or heard her.

Miss Mallard went to the spot where she had seen the tire tracks. There she strung her yarn between two trees. Then she went back to her hammock and waited.

At midnight the jungle horn

sounded again. Everyone awoke with a start. Again the headless demon came charging through camp.

"Be calm, everyone!" Miss Mallard cried. "There is nothing to fear."

The headless demon tore around the campfire and then headed for the spot where it had vanished before.

But as soon as it got there, the demon was knocked off the armadillo by the yarn.

It fell to the ground with a crash.

"Grab him!" cried Miss Mallard.

Everyone ran to the demon, who was tangled in the yarn.

Miss Mallard reached down and flipped open the demon's cloak.

"Meet the demon," she said to everyone.

"Harold Scoter!" everyone cried.

"Yes, Harold Scoter," said Miss Mallard. "**Alias** Oscar Scoter, a crooked archaeologist. He knows

all about Kimbu Tacka. He's been here before. He has been secretly digging for the treasure of the lost city!"

Everyone gasped!

Miss Mallard went on. "I discovered it today. His devilish tricks, like making the bridge collapse, and his constant complaints were all attempts to ruin this expedition."

They all turned to look at Scoter.

"He wanted to keep us away

from Kimbu Tacka," said Miss Mallard. "And to keep us from finding out about the treasure."

Scoter hissed! Then he snarled, "How did you find out about me?"

Miss Mallard answered, "I remembered that you corrected Dr. Dusty Duck about the Mayan calendar. And that gave me the clue that you were an archaeologist posing as a tourist, and that you had been here before."

Miss Mallard paused before

she continued. "My clipping file told me your identity. Then it was just a matter of catching you on your phony armadillo."

"Aha!" cried Victor. "So that's why Scoter was out of breath when we uncovered him in his hammock. He wasn't smothering. He had just returned from racing on his bicycle."

"That's right!" declared Miss Mallard. "But that's the last racing he'll do for a long time, once he's in jail."

“**Hooray!** What a story for my newspaper!” cheered Hester Spoonbill. “Dr. Dusty Duck, can you give me a quote I can use?”

“These things happen,” replied Dr. Dusty Duck.

QUACK!
QUACK!
QUACK!
QUACK!

Word List

alias (AY·lee·us): Also known as; also named

clammy (KLA·mee): Damp and cold to the touch

collapse (kuh·LAPS): To fall down or cave in

departure (dih·PAR·chur): The act of leaving to start a journey

destroyed (dih·STROID): Damaged or ruined

expedition (ek·spi·DIH·shun): A journey people take to explore something new

muttering (MUH·ter·ing): Speaking quietly, almost talking to oneself

plundered (PLUHN·derd): Stole something by force

retorted (re·TORT·ed): Answered in a quick, angry way

sarcastically (sahr·KA·stik·lee): Saying something in a way that is mocking

smothered (SMUHTH·erd): Covered something so that it doesn't move or grow

threatening (THRET·ning): Having a frightening manner

undercurrent (UHN·der·KUR·ent): A flow of water that moves below the sea or river

understatement (UHN·der·STATE·muhnt): Describing things in a way that makes them seem less important

Questions

1. Why did Harold Scoter think the expedition was haunted?
2. Did you think it was? Why or why not?
3. Did you suspect anyone else on the trip of being the demon?
4. How many times does Dr. Dusty Duck say, "These things happen?"
5. How many different kinds of bird names can you find in this story?

Acknowledgments

My deepest thanks and appreciation go to Jon Anderson, president and publisher of Simon & Schuster Children's Books, and his talented team: Karen Nagel, editor; Karin Paprocki, art director; Nina Simoneaux, designer; Katherine Devendorf, managing editor; Bernadette Flinn, production manager; Tricia Lin, editorial assistant; and Richard Ackoon, executive coordinator;

for launching these incredible editions of my Miss Mallard Mystery books for today's young readers.